Raccoon on the Moon

Written By
Bruce Witty

Illustrated By
John Sandford

Coloring
Gail L. Suess

This is the story
of a fat old raccoon
who one night jumped
way up to the moon.

That old raccoon would come around each night to have a little fun by the back porch light.

He would waddle right up
to the old wood pile
and knock over logs
with a great big smile.

Looking for food
was his great delight.
He took a whole pie
from the kitchen window
one night.

He also ate birdseed
when he was in the mood.
But most of the time,
he just played with his food.

That raccoon made a mess,
and that made me mad.
So I bought a watchdog
and named him Bad.

Bad guarded the yard
as a good dog should.
If that raccoon came around,
Bad would scare him good.

Then one night,
when Bad was asleep,
the raccoon sneaked into the yard
without making a peep.

The raccoon climbed up
into the old birdbath
that sat by the porch
at the end of the path.

The raccoon splashed around
like a child at play.
He didn't see Bad
sneaking up his way.

Bad barked out
a deep, deep roar.
It was a sound the raccoon
had never heard before.

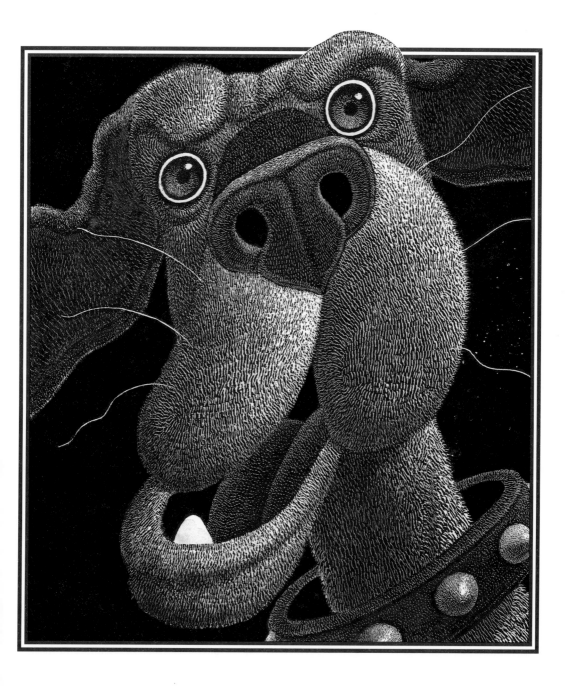

Bad gave that raccoon
an awful fright.
The raccoon jumped straight up,
out of sight.

The raccoon jumped up
to the moon, some folks say.
He's never been back here
since that day.

So late at night,
when you look at the moon,
keep your eyes open
for that old raccoon.

Can that old raccoon
really be on the moon?